THE

THIRD BOOK

THE

THIRD BOOK

by

ISAAC IZIKEN

]Elementá[

ISAAC IZIKEN

The Third Book

Published by]Elementá[– Sweden

www.elementa-selection.com

ISBN 978-91-87751-38-7

]Elementá[is a Wisehouse Imprint.

© Wisehouse 2014 – Sweden

www.wisehouse-publishing.com

*Dedicated to my parents Mr Jackson E Iziken
and Mrs Bolanle Iziken*

Contents

The Hill Houses   9

Tess and Biel River   17

The Money Lender   25

New Home   31

The Discovery   37

The Meeting   43

The Quest   57

The Third Book   63

Visit to Edinburgh   75

Love and Fiasco   83

The Exposed   89

Love Acceptance   103

Unexpected Journey   109

Characters in the book   123

THE HILL HOUSES

I was not confused as they thought; I was simply trying to understand this life, and I now know life today much better than my mother ever knew it. I had taught me that whosoever has done away with prejudices truly understands life. I thought to myself. Just then, I heard movement at the door, and I asked Donna to go and see who it was. She came back a few seconds later and said "there was a young man there; he said he came to see Gaffer but Gaffer was not at home, he said on his way somebody told him to come here and ask for him… He also said he came from Burntisland."

"Oh! I will be with him shortly" I said; and she went back to tell the person. I immediately got up to go and see who this person was. The stranger showed me the parcel that he came to deliver to Gaffer, but no one was at his house. I told him he could leave it with me if he would like; that I would make sure Gaffer gets it. I also offered him a drink and some food, but he politely turned it down. We waved him goodbye at the doorway when he was set to leave for Burntisland, and then I went back to continue with my writing. I had seated for some minutes and didn't realize I hadn't been writing, until I heard "Ma… Are you alright?" Donna asked. I turned to the right to see her, and smiled. "I have been standing beside you for almost two minutes, and you did not notice, I first thought you were writing, but you just kept staring at the wall", she said… as she walked closer and sat on the floor next to me. I placed my hand on her forehead and pushed her hair back; she was right! Successions of thoughts from my past frequently find me lost in a daydream, and I can't help it. "I am all right my dear" I replied.

Hmm … Burntisland! The town's name takes me back down memory lane, whenever it is mentioned. Although I am originally from here at 'Belhaven' a small village at 'Dunbar' in East Lothian on the southeast coast of Scotland; but despite the fact that I am not from Burntisland, and actually have been there only twice, the truth is that my biography will not be completed if Burntisland is left out of it.

I think the distance between Burntisland and Belhaven was like 28 miles now that more roads have been constructed, but it used to be more by boat in those days. Natives in Belhaven widely practice fishing and agriculture, but we stick to a small farming in my family.

By the way, of all the houses at our village there are two very good ones that stand out from others. The church mission house rated as good, but not to be compared with the two hill houses as everyone in the village would describe them because both two good houses were built on hilltops and were designed very differently from all others in the village. They were bigger, and you do not need to be told of the caliber of people that would live in such a house before you know it was a rich man's house. Everyone can easily see the two houses from any location in the village. One is at the top of the right of the hill; the other is on the Left side of the hill top. I grew up to know the hill house on the right side, but I knew when the owner of the hill house on the left bought that property from the previous owner and rebuilt it within two to three months; everybody in the village knew about it. I remember that I was pregnant with William at the time they knocked down the old structure and started rebuilding it. But even since then, you hardly saw the owner around; rumor has it that he often travels for up to one to two years for business, sometimes more before he would come back home, stay for a short while and go back again. But we knew he was a friend of 'Gaffer' the owner of the hill house on the right; although we didn't know much about their friendship, but you know… 'The rich usually knows themselves don't they?'

I always remember that my mother forbids me from having anything to do with the people in the two hill houses, and I never had a chance to ask her the reason. Nevertheless, the owner of the hill house on the right 'Gaffer' is believed to be a kind person in our village; maybe because of his late parent's history in the village that I don't know too much about either. And you hardly see him around too. But during the Christmas season, he sends out food, gifts and money to almost all the houses in the village, but anytime his servants deliver the gifts to our house they would also warn that we should not bother to come to their house to show any appreciation. At times, my mother would not want us to either use the gifts or eat the food they have brought, but such desire doesn't last at our house because we could hardly afford such quality of food, so we needed it.... At some point I began to wonder more why my late mother didn't like those people, the way she reacted at the mention of anything that concerned them at our home. I have a painting of my father placed in the living room area of our house, and I also know his grave in our backyard, and thus sure we weren't related to the people living at those big houses.

Well! Let me tell my story from where it's befitting before your conjecture about me. William turned ten a day before the day he accused me of always promising that the next birthday would be better than the one before, which I will get him a better gift... "It is another one now" he said. I told him I knew, and I shall fulfill my promise to him that year, despite the passing of his birthday. I suggested to him that we should wait to round it all up and have a big party on Whuppity Scoorie Day, because it would be a fun filled day for us here too, or we can save money to go and see Enrico Cocozza's film at Dunbar together in December. He looked at me in silence for about one or two minutes as little as he was at the time, nodded his head and said Okay! 'That is my son'… I said. He then went outside to play. Although it was obvious on his face that my excuse did not convince him, but he just didn't want me to feel bad; that was the way he acted sometimes like an adult.

It was the rainy season, but the weather looked all right at that particular time when William came to see me in the yard a few minutes later with two other children I knew from the village. They were all going to pick Shropshire Prunes. Once in a while, he tries to mingle with the other children in the village. I never allowed him to go too far from the house by himself, but I eventually let him go on that day. It was a decision I made out my empathetic nature in order not to make William feel bad that day, but I paid for it. I asked the boys where they wanted to go and pick from, and they both echoed "Tass!" Tass is not far away from our house, but I never let him go by himself either. I told them to make sure they returned on time as soon as they've picked few fruits, and not to play on the way at all. There are more damsons and other fruit trees near Biel River, which is way down from our home

that I have a history with, however, if is there they said
they were going, I won't allow them to go.

TESS AND BIEL RIVER

It seemed they had been gone for some time before the cloud began to gather in the sky. I hope these children have noticed the change of weather and start making their way home now… I thought to myself. I expected to hear him announce his arrival at any time from then. Light wind started to blow outside, then weather suddenly became blistery, where one would need to cover up their barns and withdrew their flocks and children from outside. I left what I was doing and started taking our washed clothes from the line outside, and at the same time, I got ready to go and bring William if I didn't hear him return within the next few minutes. I hadn't finished taking things inside the house before the rain started falling, and I had to forget everything and go and look for William.

The rain became heavy and strong winds started to blow after just a few minutes on the way searching for

William, I thought I would probably meet them half way but I didn't, and my speed increased as I ran towards Tess. I didn't know what to think at that moment, but I felt my blood pressure rise. I continued to call out his name, hoping he would hear and answer from somewhere along the way or perhaps somebody would hear me calling him and responded. It was not that I expected anything bad to happen, but I was just not sure what could have prevented me from meeting them half way in that weather. I could see almost all of Tess from the distance I reached, but couldn't see them. I looked everywhere there, but they were nowhere to be found.

After a few minutes of perambulating Tess in the rain searching for them, my instinct told me to go and look for them at Biel River; which is the place with a variety of fruit trees... they might have decided to go there without me knowing. I headed for Biel River; I didn't know where the strength came from, but I was running as a mad woman in the rain at the time, with high winds, tossing things all over the place, there were lightning flash and the rumbling of thunder. But I had to brace myself and continue to run towards Biel. Biel is a bushy area on the outskirts of the village, filled with trees. It is normally a quiet area on a good day. The strong wind that day made it difficult for me to see clearly as I ran… I was almost there, and still no sign of them or anyone coming from the river side. I was so worried at that time, and I got exhausted and began losing strength; I struggled to move, but I tried and continue to call William at the top of my voice.

As I approached the river, I knew there was no way they would have stayed there in that type of rain. I started crying as I kept calling his name, looking all over the place for them at the riverbank and found no one. I didn't know what to think again; I ran Biel to and fro crying.

I then decided to run back to the village and seek help. I ran from the river a short while, when it seemed I heard somebody's voice; it stopped me in my tracks, the rain and wind blowing the trees made it difficult for me to hear properly the direction the voice came from or what it said. I called out William's name over and over again from the same location, and then I heard that voice that it seemed I waited an eternity to hear; "Mother" he responded to my call with a faint voice. I knew immediately is William's voice, but at first I didn't get the actual location of where he had called. I shouted 'Yes William!' Where are you? I didn't even know what he said to answer that, but as soon as I heard the voice again, I located him and ran to him. He seemed to rise from what appeared to be a sitting position. He put his right hand on his head and I then quickly carried him when I reached him. I squeezed him close to me in relief. What happened? I asked.

He said they were coming home when it was about to start raining, and the wind was blowing hard. His own fruits fell off as they were running, and he decided to go back for them while his peers continued running home, he finished collecting his fruits and was just about to run home again when a tree branch fell on his head. He remembered that he saw a tree falling towards him as he ran, but didn't know what happened afterward. "Oh, thank God!" I said. I knew then that he has been unconscious for some time, and lucky he made it through the day.

I told him he would be alright, and I will treat his head when we get home, as we started to walk home. While on our way, the rain seems to be stopping, but the damage was already caused in most of the areas we passed. However, we were a few steps away from home when I noticed the coconut tree in front of our house had fallen which made the whole place look different... So I thought! But after a few steps more forward, I realized the roof of our house was gone. I was bewildered for a moment at the sight of it; I could not believe my eyes. I told William to look what happened. I didn't want to add to his suffering, but he was the only person available and one I would share our unfortunate wretched life, and he was shocked himself. We both went inside our damaged house and started collecting our things together which has all wet. Neighbors urged us to stay at their place for the night which I had no choice than to acceptthe offer. We manage to put up a temporary roof to cover some parts of our house two days later with the help of some of the other villagers who contributed in various ways to help us put the roof up.

We continued life in the new fate that we were caught in. We lived in it like that for nine months since the incident happened, and we seem to have gradually adapted well. If wishes do come true I would have wished that things remained this way... But the tide turned against me again when I least expected it. William and I had just finished eating in that cool

Thursday afternoon; it was a day I never wished even my enemies to experience in a million years. William had gone back to continue with his clay crafting at the back yard after he finished eating. He had shown interest and skills in creative arts, he seemed to have a passion for it, so I didn't hold him back from doing what he loved doing, I just hoped for the best for him in the future.

"Elian" I heard someone called my name from outside the house suddenly. The tone of his voice sounded as if something was wrong; I quickly got up and looked at William at the backyard… I saw him; then I went back to see who had called my name from outside.

My first name is Elian, but I hardly ever heard anyone call me by that name since my mother died. I was almost eight months pregnant with William when she passed away. Anyway, the person that called me turned out to be 'Ed' the fisherman. Ed is known to my mother well when she was alive, he sometimes brings us fish then, and he's the only person that I could say was close to my mother at that time. When I got pregnant then, I remember he came to ask who is responsible, but I didn't mind him. I hadn't seen him for a while since now. He then said he came to tell me that Fardin is around!

My head becomes heavy as he mentioned the name, and my legs start to shake on the ground almost immediately when he said it. And then he said "I just saw his boat arriving, and I know he would be at your place too… So I've come to warn you, if you know you don't have his money yet… Just run with your son. If not, somebody will have to pay him or else he will let hell loose when he gets here this time." But… but what can I do? You know my predicaments lately! I replied stammering. I will explain to him when he comes, I know he helped me, and I will pay him back. I said. Ed looked at me in the eyes and said… "Fardin is no friend to anyone; actually you should consider him as an implacable enemy. Since he told you the last time that he will get his money the next time he comes around, Hmm"… Ed went silent, then walked few steps to come closer to me; he has never been that close before, then he said, "Elian! If you don't have the money ready to pay him, run" and then he turns to leave. I wanted to say something again, but Ed interrupted it and said "I warned you" then he heads out. I wanted to stop him as he heads out to ask him not to go, but nothing came to my mind to be the reason not to let him leave my house. Fear grips me gradually as Ed's last statements echoed in my ear. I became restless; I wanted to run, but how quick would I be able to run to the forest with my son, I became confused.

The Money Lender

Fardin was a kind of evil money lender that comes to Belhaven for his money lending business, his shady loans and land deals has resulted in him owning more than thirteen percent of all the land in our community. The lands were majorly repossessed from their owners who failed to pay back debts within an agreed period; despite having a substantial length of time to do so before he came to collect his money. Almost half of our village men and women had borrowed money from him in the past, news of his arrival spread through the village almost immediately his boat is often seen at the village shore. People dispersed all over, while some natives ran towards his boat to welcome him as they had waited to get loans from him for meeting their needs. Some started to worry while others ran away... Some ran to the forest and stayed there until they got news of his departure.

Fardin was that fearsome enemy that you couldn't survive without; it had always been that way.

I'm usually one of them that got freaked out at his arrival ever since I came to realized that he was the one that loaned me money to bury my mother at the time she died. I really didn't know how I got in touch with him at the time, but I knew it was one of his boys that brought the money to me that day. He said Fardin had sent him to tell me that it was the amount he could borrow me, and I was completely surprised! I really never saw him before that time, and I didn't even go to him to ask for the money, but it came at the right timing, and I couldn't refuse it. Later in the week after, I found out that it was Ed that had masterminded the deal on my behalf without consulting me, but I'm unable to complain because it served me well at the time.

I thought I was lucky with Fardin, because years later that he came to the village again and sent one of his boys to come and get the back money from me, I told them the absolute truth; that I needed more time to pay it back, and it was almost five years after, and he has since never bothered me when he comes to the village. Although he sent message to me the last time he came to the village that he would collect his money when he next came. Many times I have struggled to save up money from the vegetables that I sold in order to pay him back but we always end up spending it on one thing or the other with the hope that I'll be able to arrange another few again before he comes. Most natives believed I was very lucky to keep Fardin at bay that long without paying him back and without him doing anything disastrous to me.

Well! By the time thought of what Fardin is capable of doing to me sank, I want to grab William and run, but unfortunately, it was too late for me to make a decision. As soon as we are about to step outside our house I saw two of Fardin's boys by the entrance. They must have come to my place first as they arrived at the village, I thought. "We are here to collect the money you owe!" one of them said.

Err… 'I was just coming to meet him' I said as I began to stammer. "He doesn't want to see you" he said. Ok… just tell me where I can find him! I replied. The huge man cuts in saying "He's already in his boat, we're done in the village and about to leave, and he said he didn't want to see you"… "But I want to tell him myself what happened!" I replied. Then they started to laugh, and one of them moved closer to me without warning and I hit him hard on the face. He got hold of both my hands together; I saw William attacking him before the other one carried him away. I screamed with all my strength whilst William's screams were vibrating in my head as he was being taking away. It all happened so quickly, and the last words I heard before the guy hits me on the jaw were "when you get the money, come to get your boy!" I can't forget that. When I woke up it was like a building had been placed on top of my head. Some natives were beside me when I opened my eyes; they tried to console me, telling me that I shouldn't worry too much that I was going to get my son back. I was screaming and struggling to get up, but they held me down, in the process... I bit their hand and began to attack them until I was exhausted and then started to cry.

I was still in agony over what had happened the next day; I was crying alone when I saw people that I never expected to see at my house, both men and women in their numbers coming to my house. Then, I got a little confused! I knew that no matter what it takes, I was going to get my son back! But why so many people came to me? I began to think in my mind, as they approached… just then, I noticed some women following who were crying, there were just too many of them who had come to encourage me to know that I would get my son back! Hundreds of thoughts were running through my brain at the same time; by then I couldn't even cry anymore; I just waited and wondered what was going on. Some of them hugged me and were crying, and I could not hold it anymore, but pushed those hugging me away and shouted at them… "What happened?"

Then I began to realize what dreadful tragedy had taken place, it was partially caused by some nature forces… The continuous rain from previous days had caused exceptional tides to raise, and Fardin's boat had not made it through the sea that night, and everyone on board had perished with the boat, I was told.

I stopped living on that day! I had lost all. After first hearing the news… My life stood still, and I couldn't cry anymore. It was indescribable moments. The natives pestered me to come and stay at their place for some time, but I refused. Some had stayed with me until very late that night and the following nights before they went back to their homes. My eyes were wide open every day and night after, I could not sleep neither could I eat nor drink. Natives brought me food daily but nothing mattered to me anymore; I just couldn't comprehend what happened. I became weaker and weaker by the day and in continuous deep sorrow until that day Gaffer walked into my life.

NEW HOME

It had been six days since I had been grieving for my son alone. Then, that afternoon I saw 'Gaffer' the owner of the hill house on the right walked right into my house with two of his male servants and a maid. I might not have recognized him if he had come by himself, because it was the first time I was that close to him, but the presence of his servants made me think quickly that it was him. Although I had seen him from far away a few times in the past when he came out or went into his hill house, but never that close. He spoke with authority, but with a calm voice at the same time in a way that I didn't have a chance to refuse or protest against his words; He ordered his servants to take all my things and another to take me with them.

Well, that was it! That was how since then, I began living at the hill house on the right.

I remember that my first day when we got to his house and the maids took me to a room that I would stay; he walked into the room later and sat on the single chair placed by the table in that room, and then he asked me of my name. "Elian" I said. He later told me how he got to know about me and my loss on his return from a tour that day, one of his maids informed on the incident that happened and about my misfortunes; he was then filled with compassion for me and decided to bring me to his house. He said to me there's nothing anyone could say that could fill the void in my heart, but he could assure me that I would never be alone again. Those words, I can never forget!

The maids brought me food later, but I took a drink instead, and to my surprise I was able to sleep that night. The next morning, he knocked the door of my room again, and I didn't know at first that it was my room door that he had been knocking until he entered. He asked how I was feeling, and he told me to see the house like mine and feel free, and then he told me he would see me later in the evening, and he left. Shortly afterward, two of the maids came inside my room and introduced themselves; they talked and talked, made fun of each other, and after few minutes they were able to make me laugh. They insisted on showing me around the house. I finally persuaded them to let me shower first that they could come back later. The room that I stayed had almost everything you would normally find in a complete home. There was a wooden bed on the side in the room; I had never slept on a bed that big before, I grown up sleeping on a mat made with coarse fabric woven together… it is what most people used at our village and was comfortable enough. There were also two big baskets cases full of new clothes… women's clothing. Well, I got off the bed and made my way to the bathroom the maids had directed me where to find before they left. When I finished and got dressed, I noticed more things in that house. The house was actually bigger than I thought from the lower ground; I noticed everything in it was well arranged. The girls came back shortly after that to show me around the house. They had a way of making someone open up and talk, being around them that day made my nerves relaxed.

When Gaffer came back that evening, he asked for me; I went to meet him in the sitting room, there were seven others, four male servants and three maids. He asked me how my day had been, and I told him how the maids showed me around and how they troubled me and we all laughed. Gaffer said he's happy that I was fitting in so quickly, and then he asked everyone to introduce themselves to me. He also bought some more clothing and other things and asked me to choose first what I like from it, but I said I didn't want anything, that maybe some other time. Dinner was served later, and I think Gaffer must have watched me and saw that I was shy; he didn't say much at the dinner table and I was glad he didn't because I was a little uncomfortable eating with him alone on the table that evening.

However, it had been ten months since I moved to Gaffer's house at the time, and I had got really used to it. I wanted to feel the fresh air through the window in my room on a particular Saturday afternoon when I heard Dona's footsteps coming towards my room. How are you Dona? I asked as she makes her way inside. "I am well ma… Gaffer wants you to join them in the sitting room if you are not too tired ma!" She said. "Tell him I will come" I replied. I knew he would ask for me; he usually did whenever he was at home; he never liked me isolating myself whenever he was around, despite his understanding that I had gotten over the sorrowful part of my life.

"Ah well!" Said Gaffer, when he saw me walk towards him, "On a cool day like this that almost all of us are at home, it seemed like a good day to learn from one another or what do you think?" he said… Looking at my face first, and then everyone else's face one after the other. Yes, it is a good idea, I said. Then, Dona replied, from where she sat on the carpet sorting and twisting artificial flowers, "storytelling will be good too Gaffer."

I like Dona a lot even as my own daughter; she's the gentle and quiet type and the youngest among the maids. She come to spend time with me a lot and could talk to me about anything. Moreover, both the male servants and housemaids never hid their liking and respect for me since I had been staying there… And of course they ought to! Though I never had any maids do anything for me before, neither had I seen any to do anything for my family, I can imagine what it felt like to be a servant. However, the look of relief and contentment on the faces of Gaffer's servants was different from what I imagined. It was the type of look that tells that they had found contentment on moving towards their destiny; let's face it… It was only at

Gaffer's house that I heard or saw servants this happy and free with their masters; it was indeed a happy home.

"Okay… You will start by telling us a story Dona" I said. "But 'ma' you know good stories!" She replied. Another maid emerged from the hallway and cut in… "Ma, I have finished all my work." I and Gaffer looked at each other's face, and both started to laugh. That had been the servants' stratagem at the house when they wanted to be around me, they would say they've just finished their work… Meanwhile, I had never given them any work in the first place.

"I've been told that you're the best" Gaffer said…pointing to me. "I can't think of any now" I replied. One of the servants volunteered to tell us one, and we all enjoyed it. Weekends are usually fun at Gaffer's house because there were no dull moments at all.

THE DISCOVERY

I was usually left alone at the house during the week while all others would have to go to their allocated assignments in the mornings; it has always been like that since I came there, but Dona sometimes stayed back with me. Gaffer actually wanted her to stay at home with me, but sometimes I asked her to go and join them. I was left wandering in the house on my own one day like I've always done when I was alone at home, just looking at the fine decorations and the great souvenir collections that Gaffer has in the house. There was a small round wooden table at the corner of the sitting room by the souvenirs cabinet, a beautifully carved elephant, and a natural flower pot was placed on it. There was also a wooden swinging chair by the table side. I never noticed at first that the chair was a swinging one until I tried to sit on it that day and I fell off badly… I dropped down heavily to the extent that I hurt my elbow. It was as if I knocked my elbow on a sharp object. I sat up on the floor in slight pain, and then I passed my hand over the carpet around the area I believed the possible object that pricked me was. Then, I realized the floor was not smooth around the spot where I fell, it seems there was a small object under the carpet, so I wanted to take it out. I moved the table forward a little bit and put the chair to one side; I then lifted the carpet from the edge of the room to the spot that I fell. I saw lines like a square shape; it was like that of a loft door but on the floor. There was a metal ring at one of its edges; it looked like a bunker's door though I've not seen one before that day, but I knew how it might look. When I tried to lift it up, then I knew it was definitely a bunker's door. I was so surprised, and my mind started to ponder as I tried to think of good reasons why Gaffer had a secret bunker in his house, but I couldn't figure it out. I let it be and put the carpet back to the floor the same way I found it, and then brought back the table and chair to their original positions. I became restless throughout that day thinking about what the bunker was made for and why it was covered up that way. What could be inside? I began to ask myself questions.

When the maids came back later that day, I called Dona to my room as I did sometimes to keep me company, only this time I was trying to find out if any of them knew about the bunker. I knew I needed to be wise about how I did it not to raise any suspicion from her. I asked her many questions about the house in a relaxed manner, and if there had been any secrets about the house that she knew or had heard about, but she knew nothing of the kind. She also asked what exactly did I want to know about so she could help find out from other older servants, but I told her not to, and quickly changed the topic.

When Gaffer returned home that evening and asked for me as usual, I went to meet him, and after we greeted each other and had a little more general conversation, I felt in my mind that he knew I had found out his secret, or, maybe at that moment, he noticed that my countenance changed because the next thing he said was… "Is there anything you would like us to talk about? It looks as if something is bothering you." "Not at all" I replied immediately. I became even more restless from that time and over the following days. On the night of the third day since I discovered the secret bunker, I decided to have a proper look again the next day when everyone had gone out.

I waited patiently in my room as the male and female servants said their goodbyes to me one after the other from outside my room door. Gaffer was the first to leave the house every morning; he had a business just at the outskirt of the village that he went to with some of his male servants, whilst others went later after they have done their specific house work. That had been their routine before I came to the house and was still the same. Those ones that would go later were the ones that will take food stuff with them. I've been told that some of them went to the village market to sell food stuff before they rerouted, except Dona, whose assignment since I arrived was to keep me company when others were away. I was determined to know the truth… I need to ensure my mind was clear of any negative assumptions about Gaffer because of the secret bunker that I found in the house, which, surprisingly nobody else in the house knew about it.

My waiting was finally over when the last set of people went out. I called Dona to leave whatever she was doing and go to get some things for me at the market and to find out the prices of some particular types of fabrics of which I gave her the description. As soon as she left, I wentand locked the house's wooden front door from the inside. I then began my quest to find out the truth. I moved the small table further away from the souvenirs' cabinet; took the swinging chair completely away from my target area, and then I lifted the carpet from the edge. I went ahead to open the bunker. Its door felt heavier, and I had to use both hands to be able to raise it open. I opened the door slowly; there were seven to eight steps leading down inside the bunker, and there was a lantern hanging at the bottom of the stairs… its light has been dimmed to the lowest.

I stood and stare at the steps and the lantern below for about two minutes before I summoned courage to go inside the bunker. Slowly I reached the base of those steps, where there was another lantern on the inner side of the bunker. Then, an unexplainable fear overwhelmed me... when I wondered how did they refill these lanterns with oil that kept them burning? After moving the lantern from side to side for some time, I didn't see any skeletons or human parts, which I initially for no reason thought might be in the secret bunker. Some part of the bunker revealed small mud and concrete structures. It looked like it was purposely trenched into the place, but the space could fit in a single bed. There was one chair near the end of the wall; I walked closer to the chair. I saw a built-in safe on the wall. The visible front door was made of fine thick old wood, and it had a key hole on it. There was absolutely nothing in that bunker that I could see except the chair and the safe on the wall. I was a little disappointed not to have fulfilled my expectations of discovering Gaffer's hidden evil secret, but at least I satisfied my curiosity or so I thought in my mind and turned back. I left the bunker, closed its door and put back everything to their former positions.

THE MEETING

Everything went back to normal afterward, I completely forgot about the bunker, and I erased all negative thoughts on Gaffer's 'too good to be true' type of kindness from my mind. I guessed he was just one rare but amazing individual who derived pleasure from doing good and treated all people as equal, and my respect for him increased since that day.

My life continued to have meaning again gradually at Gaffers house. I started to loosen up more and more, and I felt more relaxed than before. Days turned to months and months into years that I had been staying at Gaffer's house, we got so used to one another, and gradually I began to have some affectionate feelings for him, though he didn't notice. A woman's seductive instinct was about apparent in me, and I quickly called back my senses. I didn't know anything about his marital life then as he never talked about his wife or anything about his relationship, and I did not have the courage to ask him; even when our conversations were getting deeper on aspect of relationships at times, he would change the topic, and carry everyone one along. Maybe his wife lived in another town where he often traveled to… who knows! I thought in my mind.

It was after seven good years that I had been at Gaffer's house when it seemed to me that he finally got it! It seemed he noticed that I had developed feelings for him over the years. We were alone together chatting in the sitting room one Sunday afternoon when he asked me what I thought about finding a man that I would build a new life with. At first I was happy inside me that he was going to ask me to marry him, I have waited to hear it, but I pretended as if I wasn't excited with his question. I said to him I thought it was a good idea and thanked him. He then continued to tell me that if I wouldn't mind, he had a friend whom he believed would be perfect for me and that he had told his friend about me. Then, I looked at his face in disbelief; I couldn't believe what I heard. I felt like screaming to his face 'are you blind can't you see this lady has fallen for you?' I was offended and felt disappointed with what he said, but I kept silent.

I am sure he noticed my countenance changed since that time because he never mentioned it again. But with time, I was also able to work it out later over the months that he was not meant for me. Although it costs me sleepless nights to get over it but after a while, there were absolutely no funny feelings inside me for him again. I just like him for who he was and I see him as a brother and father figure to me since then. However, our life continued like that as normal for two more years before the matter was raised again. His friend 'Gabriel' that owned the left side hill house which he never stay for long before he travelled out of the village came to visit on that day, though it was not his first time of coming to our place, but it was the first time we all sat together for a long time and it was because Gaffer insisted that I joined them.

I already knew before that day that our male and female servants were also free with Gabriel; they feel free talking him whenever he was around like they do with Gaffer. Gabriel was kind, similar to Gaffer. It won't take anyone long before realizing he had a good heart too. He also looked good and liked to wear cologne, and it seemed he had a particular brand of cologne that he wore, because ever since the first time that I met him, I smelt the same scent on him; it actually seemed I have smelt his type of cologne before despite I didn't know what is called then, but it smelt really good all the same. During the conversation on that particular day that he visited and the three of us were together, Gabriel told me him and Gaffer had grown up together and they were like blood brothers. "No wonder you behave alike", I said to him jokingly. Then, he asked me to explain how they behaved alike?I replied thatneither of them ever stayed home for long and that both always travelled for business especially Gabriel… as I pointed to him while smiling. We all started to laugh at my comments, and Gabriel said "what other things have you noticed amongst us? Please tell me." And we all burst into more laughter at what he said. It was a really fun day.

Shortly after Gabriel had gone, I was back in my room when Gaffer went to his room and brought out a small folder, and then asked me to help him take it to Gabriel at his house. The way I looked at his face when he said that to me, his immediate countenance indicated that he knew I understood what he was up to. He then walked closer to me and said… "Do you trust me Elian?" I nodded my head in response, then he held my right hand, and he said it would give him joy if I prove that I believed he meant good for me and I do as he said. He never seemed that serious when talking to me since I've known him. I told him it was alright that I would take the folder to Gabriel. He thanked me and went back to his room.I had never previously since I was born stepped into even the compound of the left side hill house. It then seemed to me as if I was about to break the mould. I didn't know what to expect, but I got to left side hill house in no time. There were maids at the house too, but not as many as at Gaffer's house. Two of the maids ushered me inside when I told then I had come to give Gabriel message from Gaffer. One of them went to fetch him, and one took me to the sitting room. The inside of the house was like a royal palace, most of the things there were made of gold. There were some Christian paintings and some writing in frames of Bible quotes on his wall that obviously seemed like a religious man's house, but they all looked really beautiful. I thought the right side hill house is great, but this is greater, despite it does not look like this on the outside.

Either a surge of anxiety or something else, I did not know in particular the reason, but I suddenly started feeling feverish and cold. Gabriel came out to meet me at the sitting room, he looked so excited to see me, he told his maids to prepare a meal to entertain me immediately, and I quickly declined the idea but he insisted. I believed he noticed how I was feeling, and then he asks me if I was alright? I told him I was not feeling well. "Oh!" He said, as he moved closer to me and touched my forehead, and then a miracle happened. As soon as he touched me on the forehead, all my feverishness vanished and I started to sweat. He then said I look too worried, and asked if I would like to go home now? 'No!' I said. I don't know where that came from inside me. He said he would like to show me round the house, and I followed him. He told me about each of the paintings in his house and asked his maid to call all other maids to come and meet me. He showed me many things. That day he made me feel like a princess that came to visit him. When it was time to eat, the table setting was like we were about to have a festival feast.

After sometime, I was beginning to enjoy his treats and his company. At times during our conversations he would call one of the maids to testify about what he had told me. We laughed, talk and it was a good atmosphere. He asked his maids to excuse us, and then the topic changed when he opened his mind and said he liked me and would want me to be his wife someday. But he said he would give me time to go and think about it before I made my decision. He also added that he would not travel to do anything until he got a response from me. I persuaded him to go for his normal business tours until I made my decision, and he agreed after much persuasion. I asked if he had ever been married and he said no, but he said he had four sons. I was a little baffled to hear that. 'So what happened to their mother?' I asked him. He said he had lived a bad life and done terrible things in his younger age, and that he found out about one of his sons later, but the mother had got married to another man by then. He told me he adopted the other three sons, but only his biological son and one of the adopted lived with him in the same house at Burntisland, and he had another house where the other two lived with their guardians.

As he talked my mind felt at peace with him. Maybe because he was caring enough to be picking up motherless children by adopting them I don't know, but I felt comfortable around him as I have never felt around strangers before. I told him I would think about his proposal, and he was happy. We continued to talk and laugh, some of his maids said some things whenever they came into where we were that made us laugh even more. They seemed very happy just like those at Gaffer's house.

I had totally forgotten myself, and he was the one that reminded me that it was getting late. I jumped up to leave and he and two other maids walked me back to the entrance of Gaffer's house before they went back, despite me asking them to go back many times on the way and that I would be fine. Gaffer had already gone to bed by the time I got home and I did not disturb him because I knew he would be going out early in the morning again.

My heart was filled with excitement throughout that night; I lie down in my room dreaming about Gabriel It was a good feeling. When Gaffer knocked on my room door the following morning, as I opened and greeted him he looked at my eyes for like 5 seconds, then he smiled and said you "didn't sleep at all last night did you?" I laughed as I replied... 'Of course I did sleep'. "Anyway, I will see you later in the evening, I must go now" He said. He looked relieved and also excited too. I must have been carrying obvious happy look from the previous night on my face that morning, which he noticed.

Thoughts of Gabriel and every word he said to me were on my mind throughout the day. The day went by slowly, and for the first time Gaffer came back home earlier than he used to that evening. I was surprised to see him back at that time of the day, but he said he came early because he wanted to speak with me before it got too late. We were both sitting in my room and he asked how things had gone at Gabriel's place that he sent me in the previous day. I told him everything from beginning to end, I hid nothing from him; then he asks me if I had any feelings for Gabriel, and I said I did. He told me many things and why he believed Gabriel would be good for me... He later asked how long it would take me to decide what to do, but I told him I didn't really know that he should give me some time.

Life continued again as usual afterward, though they all already knew the answer that I would give to Gabriel's proposal anyway. Therefore, I didn't bother to say yes or no again… my actions had spoken for me and I was enjoying the delayed reply so far. Ten months passed since Gabriel had been waiting for my response to his proposal. He travelled on several occasions within those periods, but he came back to Belhaven earlier than his journey used to keep him away in the past. My love started to grow for him too even before he first travelled after he proposed to me. It felt like he took my heart with him whenever he went away. Since then, there was always a gap in my heart that remained empty until he came back again. Within few months, our relationship had grown serious, though we were not yet married, but we have already been like a couple whenever he was around, the only difference was that we were not living together yet and not sleeping together.

He asked me to come with him to Burntisland on one occasion. Our plan was for me to spend a day there to enable me to know the place and to know where he lived at Burntisland. It would be my first visit to Burntisland, and I was excited to go with him. I decided to get some fresh fruits from the village market to take along with me on my journey. I was on the way to the village market with one of Gabriel's maids when

I heard somebody called my name; I turned around to see who called and it was 'Ed' the fisherman, I had not seen him for a few years since. After we greeted one another, he said there was something he wanted to discuss with me that had bothered his mind for a long time. I asked him what it was, but he said it was not something we could talk about where we were. I insisted that he should just tell me right there, but he refused. Then I told him I wasn't interested anymore in whatever it could be that he wanted to talk to me about.

Ed also had a way that he talks whenever I saw him which made my mind boggled each time. So, I calmed myself down and asked him where did he want us to talk, and he said my place would be the best. I looked at him in the eyes and he looked dead serious about it. I thought for a few seconds, and then I decided to take him to Gaffer's house. I asked if he could come with me immediately to Gaffer's house and he agreed. I then asked the maid with me to go back home and tell Gabriel what happened and that I had gone to Gaffer's place instead of a market.

After a while, we reached Gaffer's house. Dona and another maid were at home at the time. I asked Ed what the issue was all about after he sat down. He was about to speak when I heard Gabriel's voice coming from outside talking with the maids. I stopped Ed and went to meet Gabriel. He asked me what it was all about, and I told him I didn't know yet. When we got inside the sitting room, I introduced Gabriel to Ed, and then I asked Ed to continue to speak.

He said he made a promise out of ignorance to a dear friend of his a very long time ago, but he could not live with the guilt of it anymore. He said he wanted to set his conscience free, and he didn't care about what the outcome might be afterwards. He then continued to say that his friend and he had reached an agreement in Edinburgh when his friend Angus was alive.

I became more curious when he mentioned my father's name, my late father's name was Angus, and I never knew he was a friend of his when he was alive as I didn't know my father alive either. I knew that Ed and my late mother were close friends, but I never knew that Ed also knew my father.

Nevertheless, Ed continued to say that my late father and he got married to their wives in the same year. And after two and a half years of his marriage, he had two children. He said my late father 'Angus' had been to big cities many times before and after he got married to my mother. "At that time, Angus agreed to take me and Catherine your mother with him to visit Edinburgh just for a day for the first time. After I told him that I had never been to Edinburgh and would like to go with him sometime; he then said Catherine had not been there either, so he would take both of us."

"We booked one hotel room with two beds inside when we arrived at Edinburgh, but later that evening Angus said he needed to go somewhere, and I asked if I could go with him and he initially said yes. When we got outside the hotel, he told me that I could not come with him. And he confessed to me that he had been having an affair for some time with an older woman at Edinburgh, and the woman had been helping him financially ever since, so he was going to see her briefly that evening." He continued… "I was dazed at what he revealed to me that evening, but there was nothing I could do about it. So, I went back to the hotel room to see Catherine. To cut the story short, one thing led to another later that evening, and we slept with each other." He said.

… "Who slept with each other?" I asked furiously. Gabriel held my hand and told me to calm down; 'What is he talking about!' I said… as I stood up from my seat. Gabriel said I must calm down… He then asked Ed "are you saying you are Elian's father?" and he replied "yes"… He further went on to say that sometime later when Catherine was pregnant, she told her husband about what happened, and Angus was angry. But he later made me swear not to reveal it to anyone, not even to the child that would be born. They have been unable to have a child together ever since they were married. And because I married to a nagging and wild woman who I am sure you knew about too in the village, she made me stay away, even after your mother's death.

"NO" NO! It can't be! … Why would my mother keep such a secret from me?" I asked.

Anyway, after the whole scenario, Gabriel and I planned to go to Burntisland was cancelled during that period. And with the support I got from both Gabriel and Gaffer at that time, I was able to cope with my latest status with time.

THE QUEST

Life continued that way until one faithful day. Gabriel had travelled as usual, he promised to bring his sons to meet me soon, and I also looked forward to it someday. I was at Gaffer's house by myself that day; every other person had gone to do their various assignments for the day except Dona. On Sundays Gaffer did not allow his maids and male servants to go anywhere or do any tedious jobs unless they wanted to do so, on their own.

It was a very windy outside, and I could feel the wind forcing the windows to close in my room. I heard the wind forcefully shut one of the windows in the house; all the house windows are made of wood, and it made a loud noise therefore. Since I hadn't heard Dona's movement in the house before that time, I knew she probably took napping somewhere. I let her sometimes, especially when I felt like being alone in my room. I didn't know which direction the wind blowing through the windows could be from, so I got up to go and find then lock it. I saw from the walkway inside the house, that Gaffer's room key had fallen off from the top of his door frame where he used to keep it whenever he was going out; the wind that forced the window to close must have shaken the key off its place. I went and picked it up, and put it back where I believed it fell from. The entire people living in that house know where he normally kept his room key when going out and had locked his door. It seemed he purposely put the key there for easy access, should in case he needed something urgently at his place of business and need the servants to come back home and bring it to him from his room. However, I found the insecure window, locked it and went back to my room to try take a little nap for the day since there was nothing much to do.

That was the day I started to believe in the popular saying that 'an idle hand is the devil's workshop' and so it was when you got bored too. A few minutes after I went back to my room, out of the blue, I just remembered the bunker in the house. And the next thing that popped into my head was to go and try

Gaffer's keys that I had just put back to where I believed it fell from, to try it on the wall safe inside the bunker that I discovered but forgot about long ago. I didn't know how I came up with that thought on that day, but since I was bored and have nothing else to do, it seemed like fun and an adventure too to me.

Firstly, I went to look for Dona, and I found her exactly as I thought I would… Sleep in their room! Their rooms are separated from the main front house but in the same compound. I then gently went back, I knew that I needed to be quick with what I was about to do; I locked the entrance door to the house from inside and went to get the key. I moved the furniture away from my target spot, lifted the carpet and headed straight inside the bunker.

There are only two keys hooked together, and I am sure one is his room door. I tried the other key on the wall safe, and it unlocked the safe at once. Fear of what I might discover in the safe began to wander in my mind, but I just had to do it once and for all… for my mind to be cleared.

I gently pulled it open, and there was a big red book with a few bundles of currency placed beside it all inside the wall safe. I took one of the bundles of money, flipped through and smelt it and then put it back. It was my first time of seeing money in their bundles like that. I carried the book with both my hands; it is hard cover with fine shinning gold liquid used to inscribe LOGBOOK on the front and a blank back cover… I then slowly opened it; the pages contained various recordings of different transactions with names and places where the businesses took place written on it, but both the names and places were definitely not at our village.

Well! Now I am satisfied! I thought to myself after a few minutes. I put the book back gently again, and I was about to close the safe when I noticed something else inside the safe. There was another smaller door with a key hole like the first one inside the safe. I didn't expect to see another inner safe and I didn't have the key to open it. I wondered what could be in there as I went ahead and locked up the safe, then hurried out of the bunker, and put back the carpet to the way it was before I lifted it, and then I returned the keys to its place. Well … I had satisfied my curiosity after all.

I went back to my room and do other normal things for the day before the maids returned from their various assignments, but I forgot to unlock the entrance door to the house that I locked earlier, I later heard Dona's voice calling 'Madam' from what seemed to be from afar, which was unusual. So I wanted to go out to see what had happened, then I remembered I had not unlocked the door. Dona told me she was worried about me when she found the door locked from the inside, and had to come around the house to call me. I told her I locked it earlier but forgot to unlock it, and I didn't bother to give any explanation, despite the fact that she did not seem satisfied with what I told her. I didn't blame her though, because it was the first time she had seen the door locked during the day like that.

THE THIRD BOOK

Later that evening after we've all finished dinner, Gaffer and I talked for some time before we said our good nights and headed for our different rooms. The thought of my earlier deeds that day came to my mind again, I had been restless since the first time I found the bunker in that house a few years ago. I am not sure what exactly I was expecting to find, but I wonder out of curiosity why an ordinary book and money would be hidden away in such a secure manner by a type of person like Gaffer who could give out anything. As I pondered about the bunker, it suddenly came to my mind that I should have tried the same key on the inner safe of the bunker… what if it is the same key that opens both safes? I asked myself. I decided to go back there the next day to try the key on the inner safe of that wall safe.

I look forward to Gaffer and the other maids to leave the house as usual the following morning because I wanted to go back to the bunker. After I carefully studied everyone's movement for the day and only I and Dona were left at home, I sent Dona out to get me something from the open market in the village. I knew it will take her some time to get back, and I have also given her what to do as soon as she gets back which was actually all for me to have more time to myself on my new spree. However, I rushed down to take the key again as I have planned after Dona left home, but to my surprise Gaffer didn't leave the key there.

My hands started to shake as fear grips me; because to me, for Gaffer not to leave his key in the usual place that day means he knows about my deeds. And that would means I have disappointed him; it could have been easier to bear if Gabriel was around, maybe I might have run to him and tell him what I've done. Gaffer and his household done their very best to see me live again, they have ever shown me nothing else, but love and I also cherished them a lot. The last thing I will not want to happen is for him not to be happy with me, I can't just imagine it, or for me to appear as an ungrateful person to him or his household if my acts in that house are mistakenly known to anyone in such a way. It is the reason I have been really careful... I thought.

The evening came and Gaffer sent for me as usual, I felt so reluctant to meet him, but I have to, especially that evening. I went to him but told him I was not feeling well all day and that I already taken medicine before he came, therefore I wanted to sleep early. He asked the maids to prepare hot soup for me and some fish, then told me to rest after dinner, he said he won't let me go to bed without dinner first. Later after we finished dinner, and I gone to my room, I heard Gaffer making his way to his room, I then pretended as if I was going to the bathroom, but I actually just wanted to be sure of his actions with that key. And then, I saw him enter his room just like that without using any key, and I was surprised. I later realized he didn't even lock his room before he went out that day; I had just worried myself the whole day for nothing. Now my mind was at ease as I've known the basis, so I went straight to bed and had a sound sleep that night I must say.

The next morning, I still had the zeal to check out the bunker's wall safe. Shortly after Gaffer left home,

I went straight to check if he had left the key, which I found there. Then, I knew my mission would be accomplished that day. I went back to my room and waited until it was only me at home; then I called for Dona to send her on an errand to the village market. She was always happy to go out anyway. As soon as I knew she left for where I've sent her, I embarked on my mission. Locked the entrance door, and moved the obstacles away and lifted the edge of the carpet.

I confidently reached the wall safe in the bunker and turned it opened with the key; I took out the book from the safe and put it gently on the ground and collected the bundles of money and put them on top of the book. I stretched out my hand inside the wall safe to unlock the inner door, Bam! My prediction was right after all! The same key fits in and unlocked the inner safe too.

My hands started to shake a little again as I reached out to pull the inner door open, but I was less frightened then. On opening the inner safe, I was surprised that there were two other books in there! I took the first one out, it was also a hard cover book, but not as big as the one I found in the first safe which I put on the ground in order to get to the inner safe. I opened the book, and noticed some other documents were placed in it. The book contained some land ownership papers and a record of properties at different locations. I gently put them all back into the book and placed it on the ground beside the first book and bundles of money. Then I reached for the third book; it looked older than the first two but of almost the same size as the second. A tiny leather cord was tied round it twice, it seemed like a book of secret to me as I held it in my hand. Somehow, a little more fear and guilt ran through me… my conscience started accusing me of what I thought I would achieve by going through all of these; which are not my concern, but I shrugged it off and began to loosen the cord to open the book.

I flipped through the pages about three times, but I didn't notice anything hidden in it, despite the fact that I didn't know what I was actually looking for, I turned the book upside down and shook it, hoping that something would fall from the inside… maybe some treasure map or some sort of key or clue that may lead to greater things, so I thought to myself. I felt so disappointed that there was nothing special hidden in the book; its contents were not even typed, but hand written. I quickly put the book back as it was; I couldn't be bothered to read its content, and I returned all the others too; then locked up the safe and the main safe before leaving the bunker. I rearranged the seats back to their positions, and unlocked the entrance door before I went back to my room.

I thought I had finally gotten over my interest in the bunker, but the feelings of wanting to know more came over me again one week later. Gabriel is still not back from his tour, and everyone else in the house was doing their chores; I was feeling lazy and there was really nothing to do for the rest of the day. I decided to pop into the bunker and look through the books again especially the third one that I didn't bother to check properly the last time. I found the key, and I wanted to send Dona away for some time, but I returned to find her sleeping and I didn't bother to wake her. I came back to lock the door from inside and started moving table and chair away from my way to reaching my destination. There was no fear or guilt in me for a wrongdoing at all… ever since I knew that there was nothing bad hidden inside the bunker after all.

I went straight for the wall safe, and I decided to start from where I stopped the last time that I was there. I wanted to start from the third book in the inner safe and then the others to follow as I put them back in order when I finished with them. So, I put the first two books on the ground beside each other and placed the money on top of them, and then reached for the third book.

Later that evening after we've all finished dinner, me and Gaffer talked for some time before we said our good nights and headed for our different rooms. The thought of my earlier deeds that day came to my mind, I had been restless since the first time I found the bunker in that house a few years ago. I am not sure what exactly I was expecting to find, but I wonder out of curiosity why an ordinary book and money would be hidden away in such a secure manner by a type of person like Gaffer who could give out anything. As I pondered about the bunker, it suddenly came to my mind that I should have tried the same key on the inner safe of the bunker… what if it was the same key that opened both safes? I asked myself. I decided to go back there the next day to try the key on the inner safe of the wall safe.

I look forward to Gaffer and the other maids to leave the house as usual the following morning because I wanted to go back to the bunker. After I carefully studied everyone's movement for the day and only myself and Dona were left at home, I sent Dona out to get me something from the open market in the village that I knew will take her some time to get back, and had also given her what to do as soon as she gets back which was actually all for me to have more time for myself on my new spree. However, I rushed down to take the key again as I have planned after Dona left home, but to my surprise Gaffer didn't leave the key there. My hands started to shake as fear grips me; because to me, for Gaffer not to leave his key in the usual place that day means he knows about my deeds. And would means I have disappointed him; It could have been easier to bear if Gabriel was around. Gaffer and his household done their very best to see me live again, they have ever shown me nothing else, but love and I also cherished them a lot. The last thing I will not want to happen is for him not to be happy with me, I can't just imagine it, or for me to appear as an ungrateful person to him or his household if my acts in that house is mistakenly known to anyone in such a way, and that is the reason I have been really careful…

I thought. The evening came and Gaffer sent for me as usual, I felt so reluctant to meet him, but I have to, especially that evening. I went to him but told him I was not feeling well all day and that I already taken medicine before he came, and therefore wanted to sleep early. He asked the maids to prepare hot soup for me and some fish, then told me to rest after dinner, he said he won't let me go to bed without dinner first. Later, after we finished dinner, and I had gone to my room, I heard Gaffer making his way to his room, I pretended I was going to the bathroom, but I actually just wanted to be sure of his actions with that key. And then, I saw him enter his room without using any key, and I was surprised. I later realized he didn't even lock his room before he went out that day. I had just worried the whole day for nothing. Now my mind was at ease so I went straight to bed and had a sound sleep that night I must say. The next morning, I still had the zeal to check out the bunker's wall safe. Shortly after Gaffer left home, I went straight to check if he had left the key, which I found there. Then, I knew my mission would be accomplished that day. I went back to my room and waited until it was only me at home; then I called for Dona to send her on an errand to the village market. She was always happy to go out anyway. As soon as I knew she left, I embarked on my mission. Locked the entrance door, and moved the obstacles away and lifted the edge of the carpet.

I confidently reached the wall safe in the bunker and turned it opened with the key; I took out the book from the safe and put it gently on the ground and collected the bundles of money and put them on top of the book. I stretched out my hand inside the wall safe to unlock the inner door, Bam; my prediction was right after all! The same key fits in and unlocked the inner safe too. My hands started to shake again as I reached out to pull the inner door open, but I was less frightened then. There were two other books in there when I opened it! I took the first one out, it was also a hard cover book, but not as big as the one I found in the first safe which I put on the ground in order to get to the inner safe. I opened the book, and noticed some other documents were placed in it. The book contained some land ownership papers and a record of properties at different locations. I gently put them all back into the book and placed it on the ground beside the first book and bundles of money. Then I reached for the third book; it looked older than the first two but of almost the same size. A tiny leather cord was tied round it twice, it seemed like a book of secret to me as I held it in my hand. Somehow, a little fear and guilt ran through me… my conscience started accusing me of what I thought I would achieve by going through all of these; which are not my concern, but I shrugged it off and began to loosen the cord to open the book. I flipped through the pages about three times, but I didn't notice anything hidden in it, despite the fact that I didn't know what I was actually looking for, I turned the book upside down and shook it, hoping something would fall from inside… maybe some treasure map or some sort of key or clue that may lead to greater things, I thought to myself. I felt so disappointed that there was nothing special hidden in the book; its contents were not even typed, but hand written. I quickly put the book back as it was; I couldn't be bothered to read it's content and I returned all the others too; then locked up the safe and the main safe before leaving the bunker. I rearranged the seats back to their positions, and unlocked the entrance door before I went back to my room. I thought I had finally gotten over my interest in the bunker, but the feelings of wanting to know more came over me again one week later. Gabriel is still not back from his tour, and everyone else in the house was doing their chores; I was feeling lazy and there was really nothing to do for the rest of the day. I decided to pop into the bunker and look through the books again especially the third one that I didn't bother to check properly the last time. I found the key, and I wanted to send Dona away for some time, but I returned to find her sleeping and didn't bother to wake her. I came back to lock the door from inside and started moving table and chair away from my way to reaching my destination. There was no fear or guilt in me for a wrongdoing at all… ever since I knew that there was nothing bad hidden inside the bunker.

I went straight for the wall safe, and I decided to start from where I stopped the last time that I was there. I wanted to start from the third book in the inner safe and then, the others to follow as I put them back in order when I finished with them. So, I put the first two books on the ground beside each other and placed the money on top of them, and then reached for the third book.

Visit to Edinburgh

The first two pages were full of markings with different numbers of years and dates with short notes in front of them, which didn't make any sense to me. I went to the next page, and it only reads 'The journey of life' … it seemed like an interesting title, and somehow it caught my interest to delve further to see what was next.

On the next page was written 'I had always determined to write down most significant stages of my life, and now I think I should start doing so' Then it continued … 'I am Gaffer Anser, the only son of Gaffer Miah and Nazim Miah. I am a young Scottish boy whose grand parents emigrated from Middle Eastern part of the word to settle in Scotland. I inherited my parents' wealth at a very young age after their death; and have been able to make a success of it. Many wonderful people have crossed my path during this time; with some, the memory of them fades away quickly, some, I wished to meet again and some stick around forever. Nevertheless I was raised to do well, and my upbringing taught me how to bring out the best in all situations and I am glad I had wonderful and Spiritual parents. After losing my parents, I decided to go and live with my only uncle at Burntisland in Fife, Scotland. The little stories I remember hearing from my parents about him stirred my imagination to live with him in such a town'.

By that time, the book had gotten my complete attention; I then suddenly heard knocks on the door of the house. I quickly put everything back in its place, locked up the safe and bunker, and moved the furniture back to its position before I responded to Dona to hold on for me to open the door. She asked me from outside if I am all right and I said 'I'm fine thank you… Just trying on some things' when she came in, I told her that I saw her sleeping earlier and didn't want to wake you. Then she smiled. We talked a little more before she went back to their section of the house; the others came not long after. The evening had gone well with Gaffer around before we all called it a day.

I looked forward to the next day to arrive; everything in me wanted to see more about that book, it seemed like Gaffer's memoir, and I would love to know more about him. My prayer that night was for Gaffer to remember to lock his room and leave his key at the same place that I normally found it. I didn't have the courage to go to his room and look for it if he didn't.

The next day came and after they had gone for the day; I told Dona not to disturb me that I wanted to be by myself for the day. I said she should only come for me if there was a visitor, or else she should wait until I call for her. I quietly locked the entrance door because I didn't want her to hear that I locked it. As before, I got the key and made my way to the wall safe; my interest was in the third book… therefore, it didn't take me long to bring out the first two and money and put them on the ground, though I handled them gently. I sat on the only chair by the safe and I continued from the page that I had stopped at, the day before. And it read…

Things are not often the way they seem to appear, but it was until I actually lived with my uncle before I realized it. My uncle was cruel to me, but he'll call it his way of training me well. I left his house when he wrongly accused me of stealing a watch; he later realized that he had taken the watch off his hand when he went to his friend's house to help them mix some baking flour and other stuff together. His friend later found it, and kept it for him hoping he would come back for it, but he already beats me with his belt for it. He tried not to make it known to people that the watch was not stolen because of their reactions about the treatment I was given. Though he apologized to me later, but I've decided that evening to run away from him, after all, he had been taking money monthly from my late dad's account which he said he was using to raise me.

With no specific place to go to that evening, I remembered that I had always wanted to visit Edinburgh… therefore, I headed for Edinburgh. On my very first day at Edinburgh, I met my best friend… The one and only 'Garilow' Him indeed, was one of those people whose path crossed me in the journey of life, but stick together forever. We had our share of ups and downs in life, and we did loads of bad things together during our youth… although he used to be crazier than me then; also at Edinburgh I met the girl that later became my wife. Although I had seen her in the village before when we were little but she was from Edinburgh.

As I was reading Gaffer's book, I realized the bunker was becoming too warm for me, and then I took the book to go and sit on the steps to go up for fresh air… and it worked! I was beginning to really enjoy the book, especially when I read that Gaffer had a wife; I wanted to read it.

It continued… I was already in my late twenties when I left my uncle's place for Edinburgh; I burned with passion for big city. However, I lasted four days in the city before I decided to run back to Belhaven, and since then, people who knew me, continued to ask what happened to me in Edinburgh! Well… I'm just too ashamed to say it, but I can always put it in writing for the future.

On my arrival to the city on the first day, I thought I should cool myself off with a cold drink from the bus garage before I found somewhere to lodge for the night. There were other guys and girls of my age at the spot that I saw they sold drinks; some were playing card games and it seemed a guy called Garilow was winning because others kept calling his name.

Well, I got myself a drink and found a place to sit; I barely sat down to enjoy my drink before 'Garilow' approached me. "Please get one for me too" he said. I looked at him and I said 'Okay!' I got up to go and get him one, and then he said I shouldn't bother myself that I should just give him the money and he would get it by himself. So, I gave him the money, and he went to get his drink and he came back to sit beside me. "Where are you from?" He asked. Belhaven! I replied. "Oh! I'm from Burntisland" he told me. He then asked where I was going, and I told him I just came actually. We were in the middle of our conversation, when SHE walked in. I know that face... I thought in my heart! Then, the next thing I heard in my ear was... "Do you like her?" Garilow asked. And my response was 'Huh!' I must have been carried away by her beauty for him to notice that. Well, she looked familiar to me, I said. Then, Garilow raised his hand and beckoned to her pointing to where she could sit in front of us... and to my surprise she came to sit with us. From there I knew she's Anna.

I had known Anna back at the village; she was like a sister to Lea, but older than both of us. Lea was my peer group in the village when we were little. Lea and Anna were raised together as sisters, but Anna was adopted from Edinburgh after she lost her mother who was Lea's mum's friend, neither herself knew who her father was. Lea's mother swore to take care of her forever after her mother died; I didn't know how or when she left the village because we didn't talk at that time.'

Anyway, soon after Garilow was set to leave; I asked him where he was going, and he said he was going to Burntisland… He lived there but used to come and do some things in Edinburgh sometimes. He then asked me where I wanted to stay, and I told him it was my first time in Edinburgh, and I planned to get a hotel room. He said I could stay at his place if I wanted to; he then brought out a paper, wrote some notes on it and his address in Edinburgh, and that was it! That was how we met and became good friends afterwards.

After Garilow had left, Anna and I still chatted for some time before we departed. She asked me to meet her there at the same place again the next day as she seemed to have suddenly remembered something and hurried away without giving me a chance to properly say goodbye except OK.

Wow… dreams do really come true in a big city, I thought to myself. I later went to find the address that Garilow gave to me.'

I suddenly remembered the time had gone. I closed the book and quickly returned it and the others, locked up the safe and bunker, and then unlocked the entrance door and put all the things back in their normal place before I returned the key. I then called Donna, and we sat together chatting before the others arrived. I could not wait for the next day to come. I started thinking about the book in my room that night… So Gaffer had a wife! But he still hasn't talk much about her in the book, unless maybe I hadn't gotten to where he did yet; I thought to myself.

LOVE AND FIASCO

Thank God is another day! I said to myself in the room the next morning. I got back on my mission after the house becomes empty of people. I locked myself in again and went for the third book, and then I came to sit on the bunker's steps and continue reading it.

It reads… 'I came to know that Garilow is a very rich young man when I arrive at the address he gave to me. He owns the house as young as he is, and I was told that he only comes there some times to look after his Dad's business in town. However, I stayed at his place that night as I look forward to meeting Anna the next day. Filled with excitement, I got to the place we're ought to meet earlier than the appointed time, and I waited than expected before she finally turned up. She seems to be in sort of a hurry again as she approached, then she said informed me that she would leave shortly; I knew I really haven't understood her well but I wanted to. We were in middle of conversation when all of a sudden it seemed I heard a very faint sound in both my ears, almost at the same time everywhere seem to gone real dark and it seem the air had seized. I couldn't understand anything anymore at that moment but I believe I heard a voice in my head that says run Gaffer; after I regained my senses I saw few people gathered around me, I then ask what happened? Some of them started laughing at my question. One of them later told me that I was chatting with another man's wife back at the drinking spot when the jealous husband caught us together and quietly came closer to us without we noticed, "he gave you a very dirty slap from behind, and you passed out!" he said. Then I remember I was with Anna; she has invited me to meet her there. It looks like I've been unconscious for a longtime… I was so ashamed of myself, and I stood up in shame and just walk away. That was the last night I went out at Edinburg before I decided to leave the next day after I left a message for Garilow.'

'Six months later, Garilow came to Belhaven to find me, and we both went to Burntisland together.

We were living life to max. As young as Garilow was then, he is so rich and believe he could do anything for fun. As fate would have it one day, I crossed Anna at Burntisland again after one year of that Edinburgh incident. Garilow was not around on that day, I was at a pub where we usually go to cool off in the evening near his house when she appeared, her stunning beauty was felt in the pub immediately she walks in, I saw guys countenance changed to impress who walked into the pub, then I also stretched my neck from the position I sat to have a glance, and there she was. I quickly sat back as if I didn't want her to see me, but the truth is I have long wished to see her again. She recognized me from where she was and came over to me smiling. She stood before me, and said "Hey! Handsome" as she made herself comfortable by sitting next to me. "I am sorry for what happened at Edinburgh… But you're lucky you've not been killed you know!" She said. She refused to explain what exactly gone wrong on that day, despite I asked her many times if she was married and she said no. Anyway… we started off from then and I later got married to Anna a year later. Our love blossoms in a few months together, well, so I thought. She says she likes us to stay at Burntisland and I agreed. It was the best time of my life but didn't last long as I have wished, In a nutshell, Anna made me believe she died at Edinburgh for a very long time, but I later realized it was all made up. She eventually ran away to America with another man. She was actually carrying his pregnancy when she was with me and makes me believe it was mine... well, it is a long story that I would not want to write about now.

I moved back to Belhaven afterwards and focused on how to make my life more meaningful, I work hard on the wealth that I inherited from my parents and God truly blessed me with more.

I stopped reading the book there as my heart gets sad for what I have just read about Gaffer's wife. I put back the books and money and locked the safe and bunker; I rearranged the room and unlocked the door, and then went straight to sleep for the rest of the day before Gaffer came back in the evening and he sent for me. He knew it immediately that something was wrong with me as I went to him, he asked if I was alright and I said yes; he then said I look sad... that I must be missing Gabriel so much; and I told him I was. It was the only thing that I could tell him to stop further suspicion of what could be wrong with me at that moment. Although I missed Gabriel, but the cause of my mood was actually about what I read about Gaffer's wife.

He told me that evening that Gabriel sent a message to remind me he would be coming home over that weekend with two of his sons that he wanted me to meet as we had already discussed before he travelled. 'Yes I remember'... I said. 'What do you think I should do to entertain them?' I asked Gaffer. "Nothing much" he said... "They are good boys, and I'm sure you will all get on well, just organize whatever you like... we will all enjoy ourselves anyway" he added. I still had one more day to before that weekend, and most of the things I needed to prepare special dishes were available in the house.

When I got back to my room that night I went back to thinking about the tragedy Gaffer had gone through as revealed in that third book hidden in the safe earlier that day. No wonder he never wanted to talk about his marriage even uptil now; the experience must have affected him enormously.

The Exposed

Well, the next day was Friday and my heart was joyful again that morning, maybe because I would see my sweetheart the following day. We were all expecting Gabriel over the weekend, therefore, it was a good day. Gaffer and the rest of them had gone out again for the day. I sent Donna to the market to get some things for me in preparation for the weekend as there were still fewer things to do. Then I thought it would be good just to chill-out with the Third book again for some time while I waited for Donna to get back. I didn't bother to lock the entrance door because I hadn't intended on reading for long that day, I didn't even want to! I've decided to do some other stuff when Donna gets back. I went ahead to get the book to read for some time. When I got it, I sat at my newly placed position by the bunker's step and continued with reading…

Garilow came to visit me again at Belhaven; he was still a very tough guy and still lived a wayward life at that time, despite his financial position. I remembered the evening I hit him on the face at my house after he came back to tell me that he had got to know intimately one of the village girls in woods of the river side. There is no remorse or shame for him at all about what he done and so I got very angry with him that night and my servants had to separate us from fighting before I sent him out of my house, since then, we never spoke or saw each other again.

At exactly seven months later, I heard he became a Christian and very deep one at that. At first I did not believe he actually had changed until I heard the great things he was doing all over the cities and small villages. He catered more for the less privileged people, and he became part of almost every orphanage in Scotland. I was impressed with him even before I saw him again; he was a completely different man within that short period.

When we met afterwards, he told me he realized that he had done many bad things in his life when we were growing up which he still regretted doing whenever he remembered them, or saw young people gone that direction. He said he knew he was just fortunate to be alive and to have had the success people saw now, but that he knew better now! He told me he met with the Lord, and his life changed forever that old things in his life passed away and all things had become new with him, and since then, good things have begun to fall into places for him more. He asked if I've heard anything about the village girl that he told me he raped the last time he was at Belhaven, and I said no. Both of us tried to make some inquiries from the village headman, but he knows not of such a thing either, although we didn't tell him exactly who or how it happened, we just went to find out if there was any news of anything like that in the village, so that we could help.

Garilow vowed to build a house at Belhaven and call it his second home, he said it would let him have peace with himself if he were able to do a thing like that in the village, after the atrocities he had committed in the village in the past. And truly to his words, in the following month he bought a house on the hill side and rebuilt it, afterwards ur friendship grows stronger and we became as blood brothers.'

The book suddenly fell from my hands; I was startled for a few minutes before staggering out of the bunker. Different thoughts were rushing through my head and I started to shake. I stood on the same spot for a long time looking confused when Donna came back, she tried to talk to me many times but I was not responding. I did not even notice when she left.

I knew she would wonder what perhaps made me looked confused that much. But it was just that I was shocked to know that Gaffer knew people like that at that time that could do such evil. Well! I hadn't really told you my own personal experience and how my child 'William' came by; I hardly talked about him to anybody, especially since I lost him. But I will tell you now!

I had gone to the north side of the Biel river that fateful day to pick some Slaes and Tayberries, I was on the way back when I sensed somebody was in the forest side of the footpath, I stopped to hear the movement better, but there was no sound anymore, and then I went on… just then somebody suddenly covered my head with a bag from behind, which I later recollected felt like it was made with clothing material. His hand covered my mouth as I struggled, and one other hand grabbed me firmly from behind and later lifted me off my feet; I knew I was being carried away as I continued to struggle from his grip. At a point, he dropped me on the ground heavily and pinned me down with his powerful hands, I remember I almost suffocated, but to ignore the long story short, I was raped! And I didn't know when he finished with me because I passed out in the process. I later regained consciousness sometime later and sat up on the ground as tears rolled down my eyes, I had to gather myself together, and managed to get up to my feet slowly, and then I noticed blood stains on my clothing; I cried bitterly that day as various thoughts ran through my head. How can I live with the shame in the village when people found out about what had happened to me? What would they say? I thought to myself. I was only seventeen at that time, and didn't even know who raped me. What about my family name that would be put to shame in the village? No ... Nobody must know about this! With my shattered heart I made the decision. The biggest task I confronted first was how to get home without being noticed by anyone, but I somehow made it home unnoticed. I entered through the back door which lead to the yard, and grabbed a bucket of water from the big barrel at the backyard. "Elian" Yes, mother. I replied as she called my name from inside the house. "What held you so long today?" She asked. Nothing, I just took my time I guess... I replied almost immediately as I began to feel uneasy with myself. I went straight to the bathroom. As soon as I went inside the room after I finished washing myself and was about to get dressed, my mother emerged; "I said what happened to you?" She asked as she stood by the doorway of the room. What? I replied. "When did you start to bath after returning from picking fruits Elian?" Her question and presence in the room made me feel so uncomfortable... 'I am not feeling good mother' I replied... as I finally turned to look at her in the eyes. "Oh Elian, why didn't you tell me" she said as she comes closer to me... "Look at your eyes; it's obvious that you have not been well for some time now, why didn't you just say? Relax let me get you something to eat first so that you can take some medicine afterwards."

The worst regret that I had till today is not telling my mother about what happened to me that day! Although the news might yet have killed her, but my suffering would not have been this much. Since then, I would advise anyone that had gone through such an unpleasant situation to let somebody else know about it, never hide it to yourself alone because it will return someday to hurt you.

After the incident, it was like hell was set loosed around me. I started to feel sick all the time, and my tummy started to grow in no time. My mother was in shock when she found out that I was pregnant, but did all she could do to support me; despite me refusing to tell her how exactly I got pregnant. I became the talk of the village, but it could have been worse if they knew that I was raped. I didn't tell my mother because I thought it would be too much for her to bear, but it could have been better for me if I did because by the time I made up my mind to tell her... I never had the chance again to do so as she died of abnormally high blood pressure. She had managed this for some years before then. I still believed I contributed to her hypertension that got worse at that time but I could not turn back the hands of time.

It was hell to go through that period alone, and that period was when I got hooked up with Fardin; who I later learnt that he lent me money that I used to bury my mother and the remaining helped me prepare for the baby. Neighbors said I was a strong girl to be able to go through all that period alone, and I believed them. I had William two months after my mother died, God allowed the villagers to help me at that time. I named him William because it was the only popular name that I liked at the time. I remembered him growing up, as little as he was... He asked me about his father one day, and I told him he died before he was born and I made sure he believed it... Don't judge me for that! or which one is more befitting to say to a child that asked who is his father was? To tell him his father died when he was a baby, where he could come back to ask for clues or further description of both of us together before he died or; to say I don't know who your father is? Which will hurt the child more as he grows? So... that was my story before I lost William.

Two of Gaffer's servants suddenly ran inside the house, they gave me such a fright the way they entered. I later found out that Dona had gone to call Gaffer from his place of business; she said she was scared of how I looked and had to go for Gaffer at his place of business. Gaffer then told his servant to run home quickly whilst he was coming. They were all surprised to see the bunker, which was part of what Donna saw too that made her run to Gaffer. They all had no idea that something like that was in the house; my secret place is then known!

Gaffer entered shortly after; he was breathing heavily which indicated he had been running too. Of course, there was nothing to hide for me anymore at that stage. Therefore, without asking I knelt down before Gaffer, and I told him how I got to know about the bunker for the first time, and I told him everything else that I had done there.

He looked a bit disappointed and then got himself a seat, and he asked me to get up. "You should have mentioned it to me" he said. I told him I was sorry, and then I told him how I was raped. And that was what changed the whole scenarios, Gaffer was dumbfounded of hearing my story, his mouth fell open in shock for a few minutes. He told his servants to excused us, and then asked me what year it happened and the location; I told him everything, it seemed like he couldn't believe what he was hearing; he came closer to me and hugged me, then he held my hand, looking at my face after the hug… he said slowly, "Gabriel is Garilow" that the person I read about in his diary was the person who raped me. Garilow was his nickname, which he was widely known by, but his real name is 'Gabriel Lowell' as I had known him. He was nicknamed Garilow by his mates, when they were young and it had stuck with him ever since. He told me that his actions at that time made him return to settle at Belhaven. He further said both of them had done everything in their power to find out where I was, and they even investigated if there was a rumor of any girl raped in the village at the time, but all their efforts came to naught.

I was perplexed and started crying; nobody slept throughout that night at Gaffer's house. Despite Gaffer later having told the maids to go and sleep, we could hear them still talking in their rooms. Gaffer told me many things and begged me to forgive Gabriel. But I told him it was difficult! I didn't even want to see him again. He said many more things and he gave many reasons why Gabriel and I needed to talk. When he realized it was almost morning, he urged me to go to bed.

The following day was Saturday when I was meant to meet Gabriel's sons from Burntisland for the first time but I didn't care anymore. I never knew Gaffer had sent somebody to leave message at Gabriel's house that told him to come to Gaffer's house as soon as he returned. I stayed up in my room till morning when Gaffer came to inform me that Gabriel had come, and then I told him I was not prepared to see him or meet his sons. He begged earnestly to see him and talked with me. I believed he had told him everything, however, I agreed to see him, but told Gaffer not to let him come into the room but I will go out to face him. As soon as I came out, Gabriel and the rest of them all stood on their feet. One look at Gabriel's face, told me he felt something too. Tears began to roll down my eyes. He approached me and he said he wished he could turn back the hands of time, but he couldn't. He said he was sorry. Just then, I looked at other people's face, and there was one that caught my eyes and attention, he looked like someone that I've seen before. "Are these your sons?" I asked… without looking at Gabriel's face. "Yes!" he replied… "Alex and Will" he said, as he pointed to them. 'Will?' I repeated the name. "Yes ma" Will replied. Then Gabriel cut in, whilst using his right hand to hold my left hand; "you know the one I told you about last time? That's him!" He said. You mean the one you adopted? I asked without being able to take my eyes off the boy, the manner in which I questioned him seems uncomfortable for all of them, but he went on to answer me anyway, and he said yes. Where did you adopt him? I asked again still focusing my eyes on the boy. They all looked at each other as if I was insane. "Well" … "actually, I was told he was washed ashore in our village, and couldn't remember anything, but I had a special interest in him and so adopted him." Suddenly, I turned round and grabbed Gabriel's clothes with my two hands… When? I mean when did you adopt him?" I asked shaking. Gabriel looked frightened at that point "I think around…" He was still trying to work it out, when the boy 'Will' cut in "1961" he said. Then, I wanted to talk but every organ inside me seemed collapsed and I passed out!

By the time I regained consciousness, I realized there were many more people now including the servants in the sitting room as I lay on the big sofa with Gabriel sitting by my side. They all went quiet when I woke up and tried to get up; Gabriel helped me up. I told them I was sorry, and then I told them how I lost my son; how Fardin took him away to secure his money and how the people brought news of their boat wreckage to me that day in 1961. They were all amazed and dumbfounded. Then Gabriel said, "Actually he could only remember his name as William at that time, but I changed it to 'Will' only because William sounded old fashioned to me" Gaffer laughed at it. William came closer to me with tears rolling down his face; he knelt down and put his head on my lap. Gabriel also knelt down and worshipped God.

It all seemed like a dream to me. I looked at Gaffer and said "So Gabriel had been taking care of my son when I thought he was dead, and without him knowing it, he had adopted his own son as well to take care of him. Gaffer said "yes, and don't be confused, that is God for you."

Hmm ... What else can a lady do in this situation? You should tell me! I replied.

LOVE ACCEPTANCE

Things were never the same for me again since that day that I was reunited with my once lost son William. But decision for me to get marry to his father was something I couldn't jump up to; because each time I remember how he raped me, makes any love that I had for him to disappear on me. I couldn't just comprehend with any reason for the barbaric act that he did to me at that time that I was a young girl, because he was older than I and I believe should have known much better of his actions at that time.

Many of times people told me that I should just forget about what happened in the past, and I told them that I'll love to, but it wasn't that easy thing to do for me like they said. Honestly, the only reason that I even felt I was stuck with him sometime is because of William that I had with him. Three weeks had passed since the day we were reunited and despite that day's joy that I had to see my son again, I was still not completely happy, and people were able to notice it on me.

Anyway, I continue to stay at Gaffer's place afterwards and William had gone back to Burntisland to look after business, but he comes around to see me every weekend since then.

A few weeks later, on a Wednesday afternoon, one of Gabriel's housemaids came to meet me at Gaffer's house; she said Gabriel has been sick since the previous night, and that his sickness had become serious within the day.

I immediately left everything I was doing aside and ran with her to see Gabriel, and Dona also came along with us. When we got to Gabriel's house, it seemed his condition had deteriorated sharply; he could not even talk well at that time, I immediately ordered we took him to the hospital, I then sent Dona to go for Gaffer at his place of business.

We arrived at the hospital in no time and nurses took Gabriel to the emergency unit while we were asked to wait at the reception. In just a few minutes, Gaffer turned up at the hospital panting. "What happened?" he asked. Gabriel's housemaid told him how it happened, and further tell of how Gabriel had not also eating well for some days before that day neither had he sleeps properly. Gaffer seemed not to be surprised to hear that, he just kept silent and watched the maid as she talked. Some few minutes afterward, a doctor that attended to Gabriel earlier when we first arrived at the hospital came to meet us where we were waiting, he told us that Gabriel would be all right, but they would still have to carry out some series of test to know exactly what was wrong with him. I then asked the doctor if I could go to see Gabriel where he was placed, and he said it was okay. All the while Gaffer was still quiet; he didn't even say any word to the doctor either. I turned to his side to look at his face, and he looked back at me. I had been staying with Gaffer for many years, and I could easily read the expression on his face, it was all written over him that he thought I caused Gabriel's sickness or I was part of it. I didn't say a word either after we looked at each other's face; I just walked on to see Gabriel. As soon as I entered the room that he was placed and he saw me, he took off the oxygen mask from his mouth and tried to sit up, I then walked fast closer to him and I got hold of his hand and begged him not to try to sit up. One thing that I admire most in Gabriel ever since I knew him was his impetuous passion for doing anything that would make other people happy. The first thing he said to me there was that he was sorry to put me in all the troubles. I told him it was okay, and I was not troubled with it. He then further said if he had another chance to come to life again, he would be a better person; at that moment, I stopped him from talking. "Why do you talk like that" I said… "What did the doctor say to you?" I asked curiously. He said the doctor hadn't said anything to him yet. Then I told him that I was sorry too for the way I had behaved ever since that time that I found out more about him and my son; he then immediately corrected me that it is "our son" … I sat by his bed and bend to lay my head on his chest, I told him that I loved him and I wanted to spend the rest of my life with him. I told him to please get well soonest for me. He held me close to his body and said he would get well.

I just suddenly realized how selfish I had been to continue to hold Gabriel for his past mistakes at the time of his ignorance. I was raised to believe in forgiveness and Gabriel had shown me kindness since the time I've known the real him. After a short while,

Gaffer came in to where we were and found me still laid on Gabriel's chest, he then came closer and patted me consolingly on the back. He said I should let it go... I should let go whatever was holding me back from giving all my love for Gabriel, he said he knows that I love Gabriel, he further said it was time for me to face the realities of life; he said many roads lead to a fulfillment and achieved happy home in life but not all of them were peaceful.

That's Gaffer, he always had a special way he talks that touched a soft spot in my heart, tears rolled down my face as he said those words. Just then, Dona and Gabriel's housemaid came into the room unannounced. They looked both scared and eager to know what was happening to Gabriel; I guess they had waited outside too long and since every one of us that went in to see Gabriel never returned to the reception, they couldn't wait any longer to find out what was going on. Gabriel's maid was already in tears before they came inside, and I assured both the maids that Gabriel would be all right. Later that day, I and the maids went back home to prepared some food for Gabriel whilst Gaffer stayed with him at the hospital. But I came back in the evening with the prepared food and I stayed with him overnight. Although Gabriel insisted that everyone should go back home to sleep that night, but I refused and urged others to go home. During that period that we were at the hospital, I came to understand that I couldn't afford to lose Gabriel. I realized that I could not actually live happy without him in my life. My heart accepted his love for me with no more resentment since that night.

UNEXPECTED JOURNEY

Gabriel was discharged from the hospital later in the following day, and as soon as we got home that same day I moved-in with him at his left side hill house without being asked. Gaffer was a little surprised; he even asked what happened to me? "Why the hurry" he said jokingly. But I didn't mind him. The truth is I realized that I've been ungrateful for what God had done for me. So I thought to myself.

When William came back that weekend and he found out that I had moved to his father's house, he was overjoyed and he organized a get together party for me despite I insisted not to, but both Gabriel and Gaffer supported him to carry on to doing it. William went ahead to invite my dad Ed and his wife to attend. And for the first time in my life, on that day of the party I felt the values of having a family. Families are a source root that cannot be cut off easily no matter what. Few of Gabriel's and Gaffer's friends from another town also attended. William brought two of his friends from Burntisland, which he later introduced the girl that was amongst them to me as his girlfriend. I never knew before that day that he had a girlfriend; we never had the time to talk about that area. However, that day was a day to remember for me for the rest of my life.

Three days had gone by since after we had the party, we were still tidying up the house while we talked about the party attendees. William's girlfriend stayed back with him to help tidy up too, although I told her not to worry that we are more than enough to tidy up the place, but she insisted on staying, she said she wanted to be involved in the cleaning. I went to Gaffer's place the following day when I learnt he was at home to rest for the day; I just felt he deserved my special thank you because if not for him in the first place, I would not be where I was at that time, therefore I needed to thank him for everything he had done for me. When I got to him, I also begged him to let Dona stayed with me, and he agreed. Dona was already at my place ever since that time I moved house. Gaffer further said I should know that both hill houses are mine, and I should feel free in both houses. I told him immediately that I know and said jokingly that nobody should even try to tamper with my room at his house because I would leave some of my belongings in there too just to hold on to that room, and we both laughed. It was obvious that Gaffer truly needs rest that day because he looked tired, so I left him to rest well on time and I went back home.

In the cool of the day, William and I took a stroll down to my late mother's house where we both have lived before we were separated for a few years. When we got there, the house looked deserted and smaller than I had known it. I stood at the spot where my mother used to sit and memories of how we used to live and how she had struggled all came to me again and I was overwhelmed.

William remembered more things than I expected from him in the house too, we both went to see my parents' grave at the backyard and we prayed there. He asked me if I have their photos that he would like to see it. I only had one for the man that I had believed for years were my father, despite I never knew him when he was alive, until that day that I knew more of Ed to be my biological father. William and I both left the house after some few minutes when he noticed that I was becoming too emotionally overwhelmed with memories. When we got back to our hill house, he reminded me to show him my parent's photo that I had in my things.

We met Gabriel, Dona and William's girlfriend at home chatting in the living room. Gabriel asked me about things at my late mother's house that we went, and we also talked about other few things afterwards before I went to my room to look for the photo that William asked me. It didn't take me that long to find the photo shortly after I went inside, I called William to come and see it, and he seemed to be happy when he laid hold on the photo; he said he wanted to take it with him to Burntisland and refined it if possible, and that he would like to make another copy of it too, and I said it was all right. Since 'Angus' my late stepfather was like his grandad too.

William had gone out of my room with the photo for a few minutes when I heard his voice in the living room asking "what happened?" "What happened father?" it was in a terrified voice he said that twice. I then quickly came out to see what the matter was. At the living room, I saw everybody's faces seemed amazed and focused on Gabriel, while Gabriel was wearing his shoes. William stood beside him looking confused and as soon as William saw me came out, he pointed to Gabriel. Just then Gabriel said to me that he wanted to go to Edinburgh quickly. "What is the matter?" I asked him. He said there was no problem that he just needed to go there urgently. "Since when did you know that you needed to go to Edinburgh?" I asked. I was confused of what was going on there at that time, but he said I shouldn't worry, I told Gabriel that I would have to go with him if he insisted on going to Edinburgh and since he couldn't tell me what the matter was. I told him I needed to know the reason behind the urgent journey because I was very sure that he never planned for it before that time. William also said he would go with him. Then Gabriel seems calmed down a little, and told us that it was not necessary for us to go with him, he further said he was sorry that he frightened us with his reaction; but I told him that doesn't matter that if he would still go to Edinburgh, I would go with him. He then forced a smile and excused himself to use the gents first.

While he was away in the bathroom, I asked William what happened. And then he said when he brought out the photo he collected from me, he wanted to show it to his girlfriend and Gabriel also asked to let him see it, William said he gave it to him and just then he asked William twice whom he said was in the photo whilst he stared at it strangely, he then got up suddenly, and he said he was going to Edinburg.

After I've heard from William, I went to meet Gabriel at the bathroom, and he followed me to my room where we sat down and he apologized again, saying he was sorry for his reaction, but he needed to go to Edinburgh, and I could come with him if I insisted. I said yes, that I would go with him, and in no time, I got my shoes on. When we got back to the living room, William insisted that he would come with us too, and he told his girlfriend to stay behind in the house. So, the three of us left for Edinburgh that day.

When we were on the way, Gabriel started by saying he had not spoken with her mother for over ten years. I was a little surprised to hear that from him because I could remember at that time when Gabriel and I first started to know each other well; the very first day that we had a proper conversation was when Gaffer sends me to him, before he proposed to marry me, and I remember well that during our conversation on that day he mentioned that he had no parents, although we had not really talked about his parents ever since after then.

Nevertheless, Gabriel continued to say that his mother was part of the reason he lived a wayward life when he was growing up, and that his mother hadn't changed her way of life uptil that time. "What if I tell you that I never knew who my father was?" he said... he again added that "All because of my mother's incestuous relationships, despite her wealth"

At that time, I became more confused, and I didn't even know what to say to him when he said that, I just held unto his hand as he continued to talk and William too was just listening without any interruption from him. It seemed Gabriel does not want to talk too much on his mother's case because he kept on talking about other things often during the conversations while we were still on the way to Edinburgh. I asked him what was with the photo, what made him held on to it? He then said the photo looked like the photo he had with his mother, of whom his mother told him a long time ago was his father.

At that stage, I told him beforehand that no matter what happened when we get to his mother's place, he should just take things easy. After we journeyed for a while, we got to Edinburgh, and we head straight for Gabriel's mum's house. A short while afterward, we got to a street that one doesn't need to be told before you know that area was meant for classy people. When Gabriel finally pointed his mother's house to me that we were going, I asked him again if he was sure to remember well his mother's house and he laughed.

The house looked more or less like Buckingham palace in London, although I haven't been to Buckingham palace either, but we had all seen it photos. Anyway, by the time that we got to the front gate of the house while still inside a cab that we took from Edinburgh station, whilst the others concentrated on the serious issue that took us to Edinburgh, I was thinking I should have dressed well before I came there.

Although I knew Gabriel came from a rich family, but I never knew that they were super rich. I noticed that William was not surprised as I was, then I asked him if he had come to the house before and he said yes. Gabriel was welcomed like a royal prince when we entered the compound. I saw butlers, a chef and housemaids ran to us from the house to welcome us.

When we finally got inside the house, we went through the stairs to enter a very large living room with the most expensive interior decorations all around. Just then I noticed somebody by the window side, the way she dressed and stood, I could tell she was Gabriel's mum. I walked towards her and I knelt down by her feet. She quickly helped me up with her two hands and said "get up my dear" at that time Gabriel just stood muted by a cabinet. Then Gabriel's mother looked at my face, and she said I was beautiful. She then asked me at the same time pointed to William "who was the young man" and then I replied… "That was your grandson" I didn't first notice that her face was in tears until William went to her, when she kept silent for a few seconds. She hugged him whilst crying. I looked at Gabriel from where I was, and he seemed to get my vibes. He walked closer to his mum and said he was sorry. Then his mother left William alone and hugged Gabriel in tears, at that time, Gabriel was crying too and I was also overwhelmed. We were all like that for a few minutes before we eventually had the time to talk.

When Gabriel's mother was shown the photo that Gabriel carried with him, she jumped up from her seat and said to Gabriel "that was your father" "His name was Angus, have you found him?" Gabriel then shook his head that no, he's not found him. His mother told us that she had not seen Angus again ever since before she had Gabriel. She said although she saw him a few times after she became pregnant, but she didn't tell him that she got pregnant for him, not to talk of she's keeping the baby, because Angus was quite younger than her at that time. She further said when she later thought well of it that she would tell Angus, she didn't see him again, She said she continued to look for ways to get him informed of her pregnancy and that she had a baby, but her effort yielded no result because Angus was from another town as she knew at the time, and she believed he had gone back to his town or another country and never returned to Edinburgh since then because she had not heard from him again for so many years.

After she said that, Gabriel looked at my face, and he slowly said… "He died mum!" At first, Gabriel's mother bowed her head and went quiet; it seemed like for a very long time. Then I walked closer to her and patted her on the shoulder. She then raised her head and asked Gabriel "when? And how did you know?" Then we explained everything to her. I excused myself to use the bathroom afterwards, which Gabriel directed me to find. When I was in that bathroom I started to think about this life, there's actually nothing that could be hidden forever in life. Every secret deed will one day come to light.

I came to a conclusion that Gabriel's mother happened to be a very nice woman; she just had a weakness in the area of lust desire, and she did not hide it that she got a problem. When I had time alone with Gabriel later in that house, I told him that he had taken too long to forgive his mother. I said, "So you could forgive everyone easily but find it difficult to forgive your own mother?" He said he had forgiven her ever since, but just was not sure what to find if he comes back to see her. We talked some more before his mum called me to her room; she said to the others that, "we want to have a woman's talk" She obviously was overjoyed on that day. I learnt that Gabriel was her only child, and I understood her reason why she had kept the pregnancy at that time. She told me her being unable to bear children early cost her first marriage to end. I felt so free and relaxed around her, and during our many conversations I didn't know when I told her about my father's wife in the village, and what my father said before then that her tough wife was part of the reason that he stayed away from me for long apart from the fact that he made a promise to Angus. Gabriel's mother flared up on hearing that and she said she would go with us to the village when we are leaving. I begged and every one of us talked to her not to come because of that, but she insisted. Gabriel told me that once she had made up her mind that she would go, there was nothing we could say to stop her if not, she would just turn up at Ed's house at the village when we wouldn't expect, therefore, we should let her come with us so to be able to keep her calmed. And we set off for Belhaven the following day.

But before we left Gabriel's mum's house that day, I came to know that she had four private body guards that accompanied her when she was going out and they were coming with us also. I somehow felt like I rode with a president that day. The whole journey was quite an experience for me.

Anyway, when we arrived at the left hand side hill house at Belhaven, I wanted to send for my dad Ed' to come and meet Gabriel's mother, but she said no that it is not proper to ask my dad to come that we would be the ones to go to him at his house. Then, I sent Ed a message informing him before hand of what happened and to be expecting us. We all first went to my late mother's house where Gabriel's mother saw Angus's grave and she wept.

To cut the long story short, the whole village knew that a visitor arrived at Belhaven on that day because of Gabriel's mum exotic cars. We all went to Ed's house later and it was his wife whom I can now call my step mother that received us at the door. She appeared too kind to us that day, trying to make an impression on Gabriel's mother, and it seemed she had an impact on her at the end anyway. But after the many introductions and conversations between us all and when we were set to leave, Gabriel's mum turned to Ed's wife and whilst she pointed at me, she said "You see this girl, she is like my only daughter, and I will not joke with my daughter. I hope you understand?" Ed's wife then said she understood her, and added that there would never be any problem between her and me.

In a nutshell, I was glad it all went well that day as we leave to go back to the hill house, and Gaffer came to meet us there afterwards.

CHARACTERS IN THE BOOK

Anna

Catherine

Dona

Elian

Ed

Fardin

Gabriel

Gaffer

Lea

William

Lightning Source UK Ltd.
Milton Keynes UK
UKOW02f2215180815

257150UK00001B/15/P